The Thing That Bothered
FARMER BROWN

by Teri Sloat

illustrated by Nadine Bernard Westcott

Orchard Books
New York

To my Farmer Brown, Robert,
and to light sleepers everywhere.
T. S.

For Sarah
and her barnful of animals.
N. B. W.

ORCHARD BOOKS
95 Madison Avenue, New York, NY 10016

Manufactured in the United States of America
Printed by Barton Press, Inc.
Bound by Horowitz/Rae
Book design by Sylvia Frezzolini Severance

10 9 8 7 6 5 4 3 2 1

The text of this book is set in 18 point Cochin.
The illustrations are done with black ink line
and acrylics.

Library of Congress Cataloging-in-Publication Data
Sloat, Teri. The thing that bothered Farmer Brown /
by Teri Sloat; illustrated by Nadine Bernard Westcott.
p. cm.   "A Melanie Kroupa Book"—Half t.p.
Summary: Farmer Brown and all his animals are ready
for sleep, but a tiny whiny humming sound keeps them
awake.
ISBN 0-531-06883-8. — ISBN 0-531-08733-6 (lib. bdg.)
[1. Domestic animals —Fiction. 2. Sound —Fiction.
3. Humorous stories. 4. Stories in rhyme.]
I. Westcott, Nadine Bernard, ill. II. Title.
PZ8.3.S63245Th 1995   [E]—dc20   94-24873

"The animals are bedded down;
My chores are done," said Farmer Brown.
And as he stretched, the sun went down.

But tails and feathers swished the ground
At something flying round and round
With a tiny, whiny, humming sound.

The farmer ate his soup and bread,

Put his nightshirt on, and climbed into bed.
He pulled up the sheet and the worn-out spread
And, closing his eyes, he laid down his head.

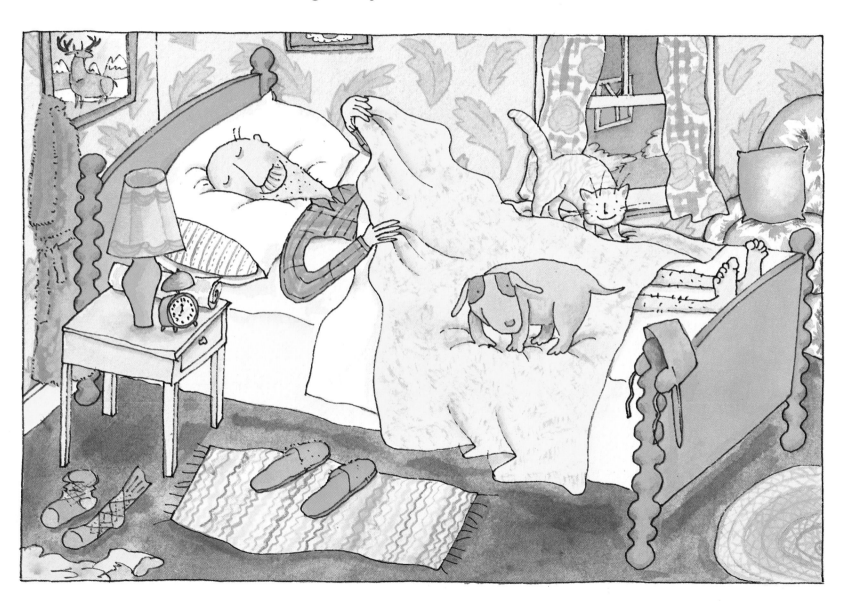

But something bothered Farmer Brown;
Something was flying round and round
With a tiny, whiny, humming sound.

The farmer gave a _SWAT_ at the wall

That roused the horse asleep in the stall
And the weary donkey, Butterball.
But it didn't stop the humming at all.

The old horse neighed,
The donkey brayed . . .

But the thing annoying Farmer Brown
Was something flying round and round
With a tiny, whiny, humming sound.

His newspaper hit the wall
With a WHACK

That upset the doves roosting in back
And the dairy cows marked white and black.
But the humming just kept coming back.

> The doves cooed,
> The cows mooed,
> The old horse neighed,
> The donkey brayed . . .

But the thing disturbing Farmer Brown
Was something flying round and round
With a tiny, whiny, humming sound.

The farmer gave a $\mathcal{SNAP}$ with his sheet

That startled the grumpy old goat to his feet
And made the hens flutter, scattering wheat.
But the humming barely missed a beat.

The old goat bucked,
The chickens clucked,
The doves cooed,
The cows mooed,
The old horse neighed,
The donkey brayed . . .

But the thing exhausting Farmer Brown
Was something flying round and round
With a tiny, whiny, humming sound.

This time he stood still
While the humming came near.
He lifted his hand as it lit on his ear,

Gave a SMACK
To his noggin' so loud and so clear
That the old dog and cat
Couldn't help overhear.

The cat yowled,
The dog howled,
The old goat bucked,
The chickens clucked,
The doves cooed,
The cows mooed,
The old horse neighed,
The donkey brayed . . .

But the farmer SNORED!

The animals slowly settled down
With heads tucked in and
Tails curled round.
The entire farm was sleeping sound

When they heard it flying round and round . . .

That tiny, whiny, humming sound.